The Second Time

A collection of contemporary short stories

By

Sarah M Davies

First Printing 2020

ISBN 978-1-71659-916-3

Dedication

To Anne

My friend since 1980, always cheering me on x

Table of Contents

Introduction

When I put together my first collection of short stories in 2018 I had no idea that it would be the start of a journey that led me to publish the novella that had been sitting on a shelf for a decade, or that I would put together a second collection just two years later.

2020 has been a weird year, and so obviously there are a couple of stories that reflect the oddity of the 'new normal'.

One thing missing from this collection is vampires, not because I don't love them any more, I just haven't written a vampire story for a while.

The stories range from the dark to the daft and feature just about the right amount of strong women.

I hope you enjoy reading 'The Second Time', as much as I've enjoyed writing it, watch out for the next one.

Newport, South Wales
September 2020

Fumble In The Dark

Shit. Even with wheels this bag is really heavy to drag along. Still it was the best of a pretty rubbish set of choices and at least it was easy to get all the stuff into.

Some choices are difficult to make aren't they? What clothes to wear, whether to have tea or coffee, red wine or white, whether to stay in a relationship or just cut and run…

Actually that's not quite true, the decision to run was easy. It hadn't been working for ages, I'd just been going through the motions and suspect Ted had been too, but when you're older you don't like to contemplate life on your own do you? And he wasn't that bad.

It wasn't even like I'd met anyone new or that I was so unbearably unhappy. He wasn't abusive or cruel, far from it really. I just suddenly fancied a change, I'd probably have gone back after a little break, but that's not going to happen now is it? That door has well and truly slammed.

I'd say it was all his fault and it sort of was, but my reaction might have been a little bit extreme.

All I said was I wanted to go away for a couple of days by myself, a hotel by the sea, walks along the shore, chips on the promenade, nothing exotic. I'd take my notebook do a bit of writing, scribble a few sketches and get some sea air in my lungs. I would have come back refreshed and relaxed and reset. I would have paid for it myself and everything. I would have filled the fridge and done all the chores before I left, I wasn't asking him for anything…

And he tutted…

Not even a scream or a shout or a tantrum, he just tutted.

And I was furious only I kept it bottled up which probably wasn't a good idea.

Never let the sun go down on an argument, that's what they say isn't it? Well we did. We went to bed and we'd hardly spoken and we didn't even say goodnight, let alone kiss or anything.

Then he started snoring like nothing had happened. He was fast asleep and I fumbled around in the dark and found a cushion and just put it over his face, ever so gently and I held it there 'til the snoring stopped and then I kept holding it there and of course before I really knew what had happened he was just dead. And I put him in this big wheelie bag, they're not joking when they talk about dead weight either! It took me bloody ages to get him into the bag. And what am I going to do now? Dumping him's going to be a bit more difficult now he's dead. Bloody typical, he always was more trouble than he was worth. Now, where's the left luggage office?

Map Making

"There are no markings on this map", she said. "No directions or instructions. I don't understand, how do I make sense of it?"

He looked at her and said nothing.

"There are just shapes", she said. "Where do I start? Where am I going?"

"Start at the beginning", he said.

"But where is that?"

"You choose. You were there. When was the beginning?"

"It was… No, not then… It was… No, before that… It was out there, in a dream, an imagining of what might be, but it wasn't real, it wasn't a place, it was out there."

"All right", he said, "so it was a point outside. Stick a pin in it and we'll connect a thread. What then?"

"There was blue sky, a green field, a tent, a hug, a hot day."

"Okay, where?"

"There."

"She puts a dot and draws a tent.

"We were here", she says, "that's where we first came together."

“Why?” He asks.

“It felt right. You looked lost, uncomfortable. I wanted to ground you.”

“Then what?”

“Nothing. We were off the radar again. There was this brief coming together, but this wasn’t our journey yet.”

“Where next?”

“Out here.” She points to the space above the map. “There were emails. I was cross. You suggested meeting for a coffee. I agreed.”

“Mark where the coffee happened. Then what?”

“That was ‘goodbye’, we were going our separate ways. We made vague promises to visit each other, but that was kind of the end, only…”

“Only I said ‘join me at this movie and you said you would.”

“Yes, but first you went away, as far as you could go, and I wasn’t there.”

“But you were. That was when I knew it wasn’t ‘goodbye’ it was ‘hello’”

“Then there was a mad week, everywhere, all this stuff, all this coming together, all this learning. There was no time to worry about the fact that you were going so far away again, there was only time to focus on us.”

"And then I was gone?"

"But you weren't. It wasn't like that. We talked and we talk. We weave our story, so many thoughts, dreams, wishes, reality. It's a cloak that keeps us bound together, enveloped in the story we're creating.

"So where are we now? Mark it on the map."

"I can't, there isn't a place. I mean there are places, but that's not really the point. There's this coming together of you and me and us."

"So when does the map end? When do we stop needing it?"

"We don't stop, it just continues to grow and change and evolve. It's the ultimate work in progress. We're on an adventure! Come on, let's go!"

Stand Forth Friend And Be Recognised

On my arse on the grass
A trite rhyme for this time
Of uncertainty, distance and isolation.

For the first time in my life I'm being paid not to work
To stay at home
And what? What?

Not what I thought.

Not writing a new novella.
Not knitting, although I did knit a pair of wrist and hand warmers for when I'm not writing in the winter.
Not playing the guitar in a day with Bert Weedon, though I do pluck a few strings occasionally.

No. I'm on my arse on the grass
Turning earth and picking out weeds.
On the patio on my knees weeding and digging over pots to plant salad seeds.
Pruning dead wood from my blackberry bush
Planting new strawberry plants – sent from my dad's garden in a carrier bag with a yellow plastic trowel – social distancing was followed, my mum put them in my garage and then phoned me from my drive so I could open my bedroom window and talk to her.

The Easter Bunny's been!
I've been popping the odd chocolate treat in my essential shopping the last couple of weeks.

I've been hiding it in the dining room cupboard,
The one where I've hidden the tin of chocolate biscuits my brother bought you for Christmas.
I thought you'd both be here for Easter, but no.
I'll phone you…

So, sitting at home, being paid by the government no less for not working, what have I done?

My garden, always a 'project', has become a work progressing
I spend hours carefully tending the spaces I thought I was leaving behind.
But I'm not.
Not yet anyway.

And, oh, poetic monologues spew from my pen and…
Oh, there I go again, recording work for remote audiences to hear on their daily exercise hour
Or whilst they lie in a darkened room trying to escape the reality of the now.

I sat on a Zoom call the other day
On my arse in my 'office', well, the spare bedroom anyway
It was with other female freelance journalists
And as I sat there, I thought "this isn't me…"

And as I drew a single line through what I'd written of my abandoned novella; like Agatha Christie, indicating with that single line, the work rejected, I thought "this isn't me…"

But as I write these words to be spoken, I feel at home, I recognise this me
I step into the spotlight, blinking…

So read all about me, or listen to me telling you, I don't mind

I reveal the little you see of me in these lines of mine
You can guess the rest and be surprised when you learn the reality.

For this is me, a weaver of words, a storyteller
Stand forth friend and be recognised...

Ghost Story

It was all she had known for as long as this version of herself had known anything.

She had no recollection of how she'd got to this place and she'd long ago discovered that whatever she did she could not get out. She knew there were other places beyond this place, she could see them and hear them and taste them; she guessed if she could taste she could probably smell too but she couldn't touch, she could never seem to quite grasp anything.

She felt invisible, she didn't know why, but people always seemed to stare right through her, she found it incredibly rude, but her naturally reserved nature made it impossible for her to ask anyone she encountered why they never had any kind words for her.

She was alone in the darkness. She was alone in the day-time too but being alone in the darkness was worse, it was an intense loneliness, sadness magnified almost to the point where it couldn't be borne, but it never quite tipped over the edge. And there was something missing, a question on the tip of her tongue that she could never quite ask. Sometimes and very briefly it solidified into a clear image and she could see the words, but her mouth couldn't form the shapes and her throat couldn't form the sounds and then, just as quickly as it appeared it faded again and she was alone.

Hers was a confined space, a closed world, even the stars seemed to have deserted her, the sky was always an end-less, cloudless, black.

The lack of hunger puzzled her as did the desire for, but the lack of need of sleep. She seemed to recall enjoying sleeping and eating but she could not recall the last time she had done either.

She also had a vague recollection of intimacy and that seemed to fire a connection to this place, hands and lips exploring another's body, passion firing explosions of colour through her mind, throat forming the sounds of ecstasy, slowly being throttled into the realisation of a truth grasped too late... Not lustful, loving passion, but hate, delight, control.

She struggled, of course she did, but the realisation of the truth had come too late for her to really be able to do anything other than die horribly. Only it wasn't horrible, it was just a change of state, one minute she was gasping for air and the next her body was on the ground and she was standing beside it looking down and being slightly puzzled about the fact that she could now see herself.

He, she had a vague notion that she should be able to place him, but she couldn't. He had walked away a bit too calmly, almost like he'd known what to expect and how to relax. He'd left the alley, something she knew she could not do.

The alley had become her world and she had accepted that, it had its limitations but it also lacked the general complications of her former life and she embraced the simplicity far more easily than she would have imagined.

And then one night she felt a tightening in her throat as if his hands were around her neck once more and as she raised her head she saw him coming into the alley, his arm casually draped around the shoulders of another woman.

He didn't have the decency to take her somewhere new, he was returning to the same spot to kill again. The woman didn't even look like her, she was the polar opposite, oh God he didn't even have a type, he just killed because he liked it.

He probably wasn't even thinking about her as he brought this new woman into her alley. He had probably forgotten about her and the rush killing her had given him... Well, she would give him something to remember her by…

… He could see a tall blond woman running down the alley, he could see the body of a vaguely familiar man on the floor. He had just been going in for a kiss, his hands circling her throat when the dark woman had appeared. She'd said nothing, but had simply reached her arm through Blondie into his chest and had grasped his heart until it shattered. And then, then, she had flown off into the stars, just before the sky went black.

It was all he had known for as long as this version of himself had known anything…

Grounded

Shoes and socks kicked off on the path I stand barefoot on the grass. If I was trying to cultivate a tidy mind the socks would be tucked neatly in the shoes and they would be placed next to each other in an orderly fashion, but I'm just squeezing in twenty minutes before I go on to the next thing.

Close my eyes.

I'm going to draw a square in my mind as I...

Breathe in through my nose; two, three, four. And hold; two, three, four. Breathe out through my mouth; two, three, four. And hold; two, three, four.

Drawing the square forces me not to get distracted, by distracting me from the thought that I might look like a complete prat, standing here barefoot on the grass.

If I feel myself getting distracted I gently pull my mind back to drawing the square...

Breathe in through my nose... And hold it...

Have I really got time for this?

Breathe out through my mouth...

I've got so many other things to do today.

And hold it...

I should try this breathing lark for at least a minute, a whole minute of not being distracted by the world... I'm sure one day I'll get there.

The grass is tickling my feet. At least I hope it's the grass and not some creepy crawly. I'd open my eyes to check, only I'm trying really hard not to be distracted. I'm not thinking about anything other than drawing neat squares in my mind...

My mind would quite like to draw scribbles and squiggles, it would like to draw outside the box, but the box is important, providing order and symmetry and calming down the busy-ness...

Breathe in through my nose...

Hold...

Breathe out through my mouth...

Hold...

And gradually I become aware of my feet relaxing and my toes snaking down into the earth, rooting me to the spot. I am fascinated by this process. My toes burrow and burrow down into the ground... They start to tingle as the energy of the natural world flows into them and begins to course through my body, slowly climbing through my legs and into my pelvis and up my spine, into my stomach, my kidneys, liver and lungs. Into my heart, through my neck and into my face, head and brain.

The energy makes me stretch my body up and throw my arms out, my hands palms upwards, my fingers reaching for the sun.

The warmth infuses me, my fingers wiggle to encourage more into my body.

I can't help but smile. I am grounded in nature, in the out-doors, I have taken the time, renewed my energy and I am ready for whatever will come my way over the next few weeks.

I am grounded.

The Stolen Sun

She felt so very cold, right through to her bones and it didn't matter what she did, she just couldn't get warm.

She put on another jumper and pulled the sleeves down over her hands, crunching her fingers into tight fists. She drew her knees up to her chest and hugged herself. It wasn't the same.

She imagined him sitting behind her, pulling her into him, folding his arms around her and nestling his face into her shoulder so he could whisper in her ear.

She blinked back the tears that sprang into her eyes.

He was gone now and he wasn't coming back. How had she not seen through him?

She knew how.

He had played her right from the start and she had fallen for the honeyed words, the gifts, the compliments, the sex. And all the time his mind had been on other things…

Not even another person, though she did wonder now, maybe he had been thinking of someone else…

He must have read about the picture in a magazine, she'd never made any secret of owning it, 'The Stolen Sun', a bright, golden-yellow sun on a dark blue, clear sky, ground. Created from paint and paper and cloth and gold, a textured treasure of a summer's day. The artist had gifted it to her in exchange for her posing for a few pictures and putting a roof over his head when he needed a place to stay.

And now 'The Stolen Sun' had itself been stolen, by a man whose golden words had turned her head and made her less than cautious.

Of course (she realised now), the lockdown had made her complacent, he couldn't go anywhere with movement curtailed and unnecessary journeys frowned upon, could he? She had him all to herself and whatever concerns she had about the advisability of this relationship could be worked on while they were thrown together in this strange new world.

And then he'd bolted, done a moonlight flit with 'The Stolen Sun' tucked under his arm. Still, it wasn't all bad, she'd grown tired of that painting recently anyway…

She opened the cellar door and descended the steps, not all the way down, she had no desire to get too close to the shambling figure surrounded by hundreds of pictures of sunlight, sunny days and half-remembered scenes of joy.

"I need another picture, someone's stolen my sun." She sneered into the half-light.

The Path Not Taken

In the beginning she was 13. She worked very hard not to be noticed and she worked even harder to be good enough. She so wanted to be one of the cool kids, but she was not one. She so wanted to be one of the leaders of the pack, but she did not have the right energy. She was an observer, an 'almost' cool kid, on the periphery, never quite 'there'.

She heard the music, saw the clothes, dreamed about making a statement, but she was never quite brave enough.

She was never bullied, never put down, but she never quite took that step into the light.

She didn't think she was unhappy, she didn't think she was on cloud nine either, she was just okay, getting along, holding her own, nothing special.

In the real world she was simply ordinary and in the real world she didn't yet know how to change that, but inside she was a dreamer and dreams have a power all of their own.

In the dream world she was the fearless heroine, not the damsel in distress, she was the practical, sensible one, the girl who got the job done.

In the dream world she wore the clothes, she sang the songs, she had the skills to make anything happen. In the dream world she knew she was happy.

In the real world she had the wrong body for the brain in her head, classically hourglass, chest entering the room long before the rest of her; how were you supposed to cope with that? Baggy jumpers, hunch up, hope nobody notices, that's the key.

The school Chapel was, like her, on the periphery, tucked away on the edge of the campus. She was drawn there, it was quiet and contemplative and there was a community of like-minded misfits. She felt comfortable there and she found a safe space to develop and explore. She made music, drew, wrote and made friends. In this place she not only knew stuff, she felt confident to share her thoughts and she began to share and to lead.

None of it made her any more the cool kid, she still couldn't rock the clothes or the hair, this wasn't a fairytale after all, but it did give her a place and a purpose and a way to tell her stories.

The years went by and she kept on doing what she was doing. She never felt like she was missing anything, but she never seemed to be in the photographs. She realised that more often than not she was behind the camera or she was off creating something new.

Faith was deep-seated in her, not linked to a place or a community, but anchoring her soul. She had never had that road to Damascus moment, she didn't need it, she knew, as she had always known, that the Spirit was everywhere and in everything.

Sharing her faith took her out of her comfort zone and gave her the confidence to try other things too, never anything too radical, but things she had thought she would never do.

And then she was 18 and studying theology as well as living it. because she could and she wanted to and a friend and mentor put a startling proposition to her...

“There’s a place for you in the convent if you want it…”

Did she want it? Could she take the veil and become a Bride of Christ? Could she retreat down that long driveway away from the world?

On the one hand yes, of course she could, she could go, give up a life of her own for one of obedience to a rule, but she had walked that path one day and the thing that struck her was that it was enclosed and the branches were all closed off. It would be like following a trail in the forest laid by someone else, all the interesting and intriguing spurs off the main, safe path would be forbidden.

She didn’t yet know why, but she knew she had to be free to explore those spurs, she knew her life could not be so fixed, she looked at her friend and slowly said,

“It’s not for me. I don’t want to close my life down I have no idea where I’m going or what I’m doing and that’s okay, that’s how it’s supposed to be. Maybe one day I’ll have a clue, but until then I want to be able to explore every path.”

And so she walked away from a life of simplicity and certainty. She walked away from the periphery and explored every avenue; some were dead ends and some brought her back to where she started, but she was in control of her own destiny, even if that destiny was always to explore and always to question “why?” and “where next?”

Down the years she realised that there were no answers, there were only new questions and new adventures; new paths to follow and new forests to explore. And in the world she found her God in the spirits of every place her spirit touched and she was happy.

Forgotten Bags

She piles her hair onto the top of her head and loops a pair of old knickers around it to keep it up. She washes her face with warm water, no soap. She doesn't bother drying it.

She clambers into the bath, water almost too hot and as deep as she can get it without it overflowing. No bubble bath, just a good sprinkling of rock salt.

She exfoliates her feet and hands, rubbing the scratchy mixtures across her skin to take away the dead cells. Then she does her face.

She soaps up her right leg, not expensive soap, just the stuff she always has and then carefully, tenderly shaves it. She does this by touch, she can't see properly without her glasses, but she's allergic to wax. She repeats on the other leg and then does under her arms.

No candles, no music, no glass of wine; she revels in the silence and the calm that this ritual brings her.

She lies back, enveloped in the water, feeling safe and supported in the warmth.

She reaches out for two old, cold tea bags, closes her eyes and pops them on.

15 minutes of blissful relaxation like this and the bags under her eyes will be forgotten.

Digital Free

Anna Log woke up one fine Saturday morning, jumped out of bed and prepared for her day.

She spent twenty minutes practicing her start-the-day yoga poses and then moved on to a hearty breakfast of granola, yoghurt, boiled eggs and granary bread.

She made a cup of herbal tea and flicked through her diary to check what she had planned. There was a small list of essential tasks, so Anna did her laundry and hung it out on the washing line in the warm sunshine to dry. She mixed up a new batch of granola and then took half an hour to start the process of baking some bread.

Her early tasks completed, Anna brewed a pot of black coffee, her Saturday morning treat, she took her favourite mug and her current book and settled down on a bench in her garden to read. She was soon on to her second mug of the bitter, dark liquid and well on her way to finishing the book.

Before the sun was too high in the sky, Anna did some gardening weeding her vegetable beds and harvesting some strawberries and blackcurrants.

Jam making took up the time before lunch and there were enough blackcurrants left for a pie too.

Lunch was a chunky vegetable soup and a doorstep of the freshly made bread.

She had a pile of mending to do, things that she'd snagged on plants or worn out. If it could be mended Anna mended it, otherwise she re-used the elements to make new things.

Mending done, she got ready to go out, she grabbed her basket, her list and her purse, she had a few errands to run before meeting some friends for a trip to the local art gallery.

The exhibition was an interesting one and Anna and her friends enjoyed exploring all the rooms of the gallery before they went to the tea rooms for refreshments and a good chat.

Before heading for their respective homes Anna and her friends took out their diaries and made the date for their next get together.

Anna enjoyed her walk home, she deliberately chose the longest route, she was in no hurry, there was plenty of time.

Arriving home she got the now dry laundry off the line, folded it carefully and put it away.

Having enjoyed a rather large slice of carrot cake with her afternoon tea Anna chose a supper of bread, cheese, apples, olives and a small glass of white wine. She took the food and her book back into the garden, she ate and read until it was too dark to see the pages, then she returned to the house.

Anna washed her plate and put away all the pots she had used through the day. She treated herself to a final small glass of wine…

The clock struck ten…

"End program", said Anna, as she left the holographic deck and returned to her duties on the starship much refreshed.

Moving

Curled in a tight ball I lie in the darkness content and warm. Do I want to move? Do I have to move? My eyes are closed. I could open them to see if there are any flashes of light, but I don't, that would spoil the peace. I can hear muffled sounds of the day outside but it is not yet my day, so I ignore them.

I open one balled fist, stretch my fingers wide. Not horrible. I twitch my fingers, consider un-balling the other fist. Decide against it.

I turn over ponderously, decide to stretch out my legs and arch my back, but space is limited and I feel constrained. It's beginning to irritate me, there's not enough room for me in here any more.

The noises of the day outside are becoming more insistent, calling me to take my place in the world.

One final, glorious stretch and then I push…

The covers off my bed, roll out, yawn and start my day.

Cassie Does Life

Cassie was struggling. She knew she was carrying too much, but she was afraid to let go of anything, 'just in case'. You never could tell when something from your past might come in useful. None of it ever had come in useful, but pound to a penny, if she let something go she would need it the very next day…

… And then it came, that unexpected moment; that time of dread.

Cassie, like everyone else, was stuck at home. Nothing was the same, all the familiar rules had changed. For a while Cassie was in a spin, she didn't know what to do.

Wait.

Of course she knew what to do.

She made a list.

She made a list of all the hurts, frustrations, disappointments, spoiled plans, crap jobs, wrong turns, unwise moves, and unhelpful people in her past and her present, and she began to let them go. Anything that sucked the lifeblood out of her went on the list. If there had been a bit of good in an experience or a relationship she acknowledged it, then she wrote it on the list. It was a loooong list.

With each fullstop she began to feel lighter, more free, less squashed.

She kept the list for weeks, adding things as they came to her, acknowledging them and saying a final goodbye.,

When she hadn't added anything to the list for a fortnight, she took it carefully out into her garden. Cassie laid the list reverently in an old saucepan and set fire to it.

As the smoke drifted away into the evening sun, Cassie felt all the armoured scales drop away from her body. She was letting go of all that was holding her down and holding her back. She didn't need the protective shell she'd so carefully crafted after each disappointment, she was stronger than that. She was a Firebird, a phoenix rising from the ashes, stronger than she had ever been, ready to face the new day.

Bone Shaker

The wind whipped her hair into her eyes and prickled her face. Spray rose from the road as she flew along the wet streets. It was years since she'd done this, but the muscle-memory had kicked in far more quickly than she'd imagined and it was like she'd never stopped.

She had stopped, of course. She'd probably thought it was unseemly for a woman in her position to be bombing around on a pushbike. It was difficult to be a 'lady that lunches' if you arrived at restaurants bathed in sweat, with helmet hair, wearing full-on bike gear… She'd adopted the heeled court shoes, the calf-length skirts, flouncy blouses, well-cut cardigans and velvet hairbands of the tidily well-off suburban housewife.

The bike had been relegated to the slightly leaky shed at the bottom of the garden, where over the years it had seized up just like she had. She'd had the drive and the confidence knocked out of her by a husband who didn't care as long as she was presenting a face that made him look good. The children needed her energy to make their lives function fabulously. And finally, a mixture of health scares and inevitable aging, where her body couldn't decide whether to shut her down, consume her or overwhelm her with emotional shit.

The children had moved on, detaching themselves from her and becoming their own independent entities, only really touching base when they needed a few quid, a decent meal, or help with a complicated laundry challenge.

As for the husband? He'd squeezed her dry to get where he wanted to be and then he'd traded her in for a model that was everything she wasn't. Oh yes: the successful woman with her own career, her own home and her own life; all the things she'd given up. Once she would have said 'happily sacrificed on the altar of a successful family life', but none of that had been true. None of them had been happy; they just didn't know how to stop doing what they were doing.

Of course, after he'd left, she'd had no choice but to survive; a shell shuffling through the landscape, slowly reinventing a person with a twenty-year gap in their timeline. It was as if she'd been in a vegetative state.

One day she'd gone into the shed at the bottom of the garden. The blue bike stood before her, defiant and dusty, seized up and in serious need of a good sponge down...

Her first bike had been blue. She remembered her dad lifting it out of his car. 'No stabilizers,' he'd said; she'd just have to give it a go. She'd sat on it and he'd given her a gentle shove and she'd wobbled along the quiet road... And fallen off. But she'd got back on and kept getting back on after every fall, until eventually she'd glided gracefully down the street and into the deep storm drain running parallel to the road (but with balance sorted, steering was bound to come).

So, refurbishing the bike became her project, stripping it down and rebuilding it as she rebuilt herself, working out, with the help of YouTube, where all the bits went.

Now, as she whisked her way across the rain-soaked landscape, tunelessly singing out loud, she was heading for lunch with new friends, safe in the knowledge that she'd only been sleeping. Her brain had shut down to protect itself, but now she was back and ready for anything life chose to throw at her.

Capture

He moves, jerkily at first, awkwardly even, trying to give her what she wants but never quite delivering.

She sits quietly, watching, waiting. She will know what she wants when she sees it, but it has not yet come.

He relaxes as time goes on, realises that she will not direct him, realises that she's waiting for him to settle into it and find his own way. He is intrigued that she trusts him to find his own way, trusts him to discover his own path, it gives him the courage to try new things and experiment with his form.

She watches, fascinated by the process he's going through, delighting in the shapes he is making even if they're not quite right yet. She senses him getting closer to what she's looking for, she can see his eyes closing, see his mind clearing as he responds to the music playing softly in the background.

As he curls up, she stretches in her chair and then sits forward eager to see what he will come up with next, how the music will move him next. Her fingers twitch, she thinks about changing the track, but instinct tells her that that will be the wrong move, that she needs to trust his reactions to the carefully chosen playlist…

And she has chosen carefully, she is an old hand at this, she knows it can take a while to get the mood right and so she watches…

She sips the glass of champagne, an affectation her teacher had that she adopted. She doesn't like champagne, it is merely habit, part of the way she works now, she'd never choose to drink it socially, but she considers it part of her working toolkit.

Yes, he's almost ready, she can see him beginning to form the shapes she imagined when she was planning this. She begins to hum quietly her voice low and deep. He reacts by creating more interesting shapes, his hands playing softly around his body.

She reaches out carefully, quietly, she knows she mustn't break into his thoughts, he has forgotten that she is even in the room, he has forgotten that he is even in the room, he is somewhere in his imagination, flying free and exploring a new world.

His eyes are closed, his mouth open slightly. He licks his lips, maybe he can smell the champagne she's drinking, there's none for him, not yet, not until he delivers what she's after.

Almost... Almost... The anticipation is becoming too much for her, he's so close...

And there, there it is...

She pushes the shutter again and again, she hears the camera click and is bathed in the light of the flash bulb. And she has it. The perfect image. She has managed to capture that perfect moment of delight and her work is done.

The Gift

“I hope this gift brings you peace”. So reads the tag on the gift I find outside my bedroom door…

I live on my own…

I don’t recognise the writing on the tag, and, given that I haven’t spoken about my current state to anyone, I can’t understand who might have felt that I need a gift to lift my spirits…

More to the point, how did it get here? The front door to my flat is securely locked, because, well, you never know do you?

My phone bleeps. A text from a number I don’t recognise; “What do you think of the gift?”

I delete it. No one responds to random texts do they? I mean, do they? Do you?

It’s a nicely wrapped gift, not cheap paper and tacky bows, it’s really classy, someone who knows what they’re doing had wrapped that gift.

My phone bleeps again; “Go on, open it, what have you got to lose?”

Well, my fingers or my whole hand, if it’s a bloody bomb.

I delete the text. I block the number. Bloody weirdos, how do they always get my number?

It's a very small gift. Too big to have fitted through the letterbox and I haven't got a chimney, so how the bloody hell did it get into my flat?

I think about who has a spare key. Mrs Pym next door has one when I go away, but I just give it to her the day before and then get it back as soon as I get home. She doesn't strike me as the sort who'd get a duplicate cut so that she can get in whenever she fancies. I can't really ask her can I? That'd be a bit rude.

The only other person who's ever had a key to my flat (not this flat though), is Ross, but he gave it me back, well threw it me back really, when we split up last year. I've not seen hide nor hair of him since then, I think he moved away soon after the split. What it was, was I didn't want to commit; well, I did, just not to him. He was all right and everything, but I didn't really see a future in our relationship, he was always a bit too serious and I just wanted to have a few more years of fun before I settled down. I mean I might have settled down with him if there hadn't been this nagging at the back of my mind, this feeling that if I hooked up with him my life would never really be my own...

My phone bleeps again, another number I don't recognise, "Can't get rid of me that easily, Jude. Open the box, go on, you'll love it."

I delete the text. I'm not going to reply, I don't want to encourage whoever it is...

It is a nice looking present though. Maybe there's some jewellery or a silk scarf inside. Maybe it's the start of a treasure hunt, the clue to finding the first in a series of boxes that leads to a big prize... Or maybe it'll blow your hand off.

You never know do you? There are some right nutters around....

I pick the gift up, turn it around in my hand. I feels heavy. It's ticking. Fuck! It is a bomb...
What I should do is stick it in the sink and fill it with water, or flush it down the loo; but then if it explodes and wrecks the flat I'll lose my deposit. I begin to unwrap the package...

Now some people, they just tear the wrapping off, keen to get to the action as quickly as possible. Me, I'm really careful, I take it slowly, slit the tape with a knife and then carefully unfold the paper, because you never know when you could use a bit of nice stuff.

There's a box inside. I open it. Sitting on a tiny red velvet cushion there's a pocket watch. Attached to the watch there's another tag.

"Jude, you can turn back time. You know you want to. We could still be great together if you'd just come 'round to my way of thinking... Love always, Ross"...

I pick up my phone....

"He's done it again. I need to move on. I need a new name this time, the whole shebang.",

The Police have been really good, really supportive. I still can't remember some of the things that happened when I was with Ross, and they won't tell me, they say I need to be ready to remember and when I am, I can call them and they'll be there for me. Until then, they move me whenever I need to and warn him off and then it goes quiet for a bit...

But then the gifts start to arrive again. Always...

Virus

"Slow down."

I struggle to get the message at first. It's not that I don't hear it, it's more that I don't listen and don't think about the words.

The reality is that I'm so plugged in to the world that I'm used to being bombarded by 'stuff' all the time, so it takes my brain a while to process an alien message.

"Slow down."

I take all the social media hysteria off my phone. It helps.

I snooze a lot of email communications, people reaching out to me desperately trying to keep things 'normal'. I decide that 'normal' is exactly the thing I'd like to get away from for a while.

The idea of being able to stop habits that in 'normal' life seem unbreakable is appealing. The idea of 'finding time' for those projects that I never get around to, even more so.

The routine I create for myself is based on having the time, not needing to rush, being in control of my little world, of my bit of physical space.

"Slow down."

And by slowing down I feel better, I get more done.

I switch off my alarm clock and guess what? I wake up at the exact same time every day, but instead of being jolted awake by depressing news stories, I take my time to come to. I get up, make a coffee and take some quiet time to contemplate the day ahead.

I'm eating more slowly too. I take time to prepare the food I enjoy and then I linger over my meals. No shoving down a snack on the go.

My house is sparkling because I have the time to give it a proper clean, not the quick zip through 'normal' life allows for, I even pull furniture out and clean behind it. I wash the windows.

I attack my garden with vigour, jobs that I've left undone for ages because they seemed too big to contemplate are now completed in a matter of hours. No amount of weeding is too much. Thank the gods that the weather is good and that I have a garden to escape to.

"Slow down."

Only in some ways I don't… I no longer have an excuse not to go jogging, so I go. I challenge myself to run 2.5K without stopping and I smash it at the first attempt. And I drag out my yoga mat again and start practicing that too. And what with the jogging and the yoga and the cleaning and the gardening, after three days I struggle to move a muscle… But I'm sleeping better and I feel great!

My job is in stasis at the moment, wrapped in clingfilm mostly, because this new 'normal' has no place for restaurants. I miss my work mates and our regular customers, but the lack of going out to work gives me more time to put pen to paper and write.

I wrote a book a few months ago. It was – and still is – dreadful. It was the product of doing something without giving it the proper time. It will, I'm pleased to say, never the see the light of day. I am going to take the time to shred it.

I'm planning my next book now. And that's the key word 'planning'. I'm making sure I have all the research done, the plot in place, the characters mapped out, before I start. I'm giving the book the time it deserves to be the best it can be.

"I don't have time..." Which so often means "I don't want to..." Well, now I do have the time and it turns out there are still things I don't want to do, so I'm stopping feeling guilty about those things, because they're too often things I think I 'ought' to be doing to please someone else. I certainly don't have time to be wasting on pleasing other people, you never get any thanks for it.

"Slow down."

43

43. It's the answer. Not to the Ultimate Question, that's 42, obviously, and to really understand that one I'd always have to know where my towel is and right now I don't, I'm lucky if I know what day it is.

Anyway, this rather rusted 43 on an old, weathered, wooden door, marks the answer to my prayers. The prayers that started when I decided to leave my 9-5 life.

Thing is my life was okay, no stuck in a rut relationship, no kids, no money worries, none of that, just an ordinary job in an ordinary city. No whizz, no bang, no pop, just ordinary humdrum existence.

One day I woke up and decided I'd better have a mid life crisis before even the opportunity to do that passed me by. So d'ya know what? I just didn't go into work. I mean I could have. I got showered and dressed, had breakfast, left the house, even started heading for the office... Then I thought "sod this for a game of soldiers!" And headed off in a completely different direction.

To make things worse I turned my phone off. Well, I didn't want work phoning me and then me having to think of an excuse on the hop. I planned to phone them later when I'd got my story straight. Only well, things happened and I forgot...

...I met him in a café, it wasn't weird or anything. It was busy in there that day and he was sitting at a biggish table by himself so I asked if I could sit there too. We didn't speak, he was doodling on a napkin and I was reading a trashy novel.

Over the next few weeks we saw each other in that same café and sat at the same table, not talking. Then out of the blue one day I asked him why he was drawing? Not what. I could see what, it was a naked bloke and it was pretty good, but why?

"I'm trying not to think about something."

That's what he said. It turns out he was a novelist and he was stuck on a problem with his latest book and he was letting his mind wander by drawing.

"Does it help?" I had to ask didn't I? I just found it really weird that he was drawing to solve a writing problem.

"It does." He said "I let my mind wander as far away from the problem as I can get and then when I'm least expecting it the answer pops into my head."

Of course I really wanted to know who the bloke was he was drawing, he seemed to have a pretty intimate knowledge of his anatomy, but I'm British and we don't ask those sorts of questions do we? So I sat quietly for a bit. Then he said.

"What are you trying to work out?"

I mean he didn't know me or anything, not even my name, and he just came right out and asked me.

"What makes you think I'm trying to work something out?"

"Isn't everyone? You're not really going to tell me everything about your life's perfect are you?"

And so I told him. I told him my life was okay, nothing special, but not bad. And he said if I wanted somewhere to escape my 9-5 he had a spare room in his house that I was welcome to use and he gave me his address…

Well, I wasn't going to go there was I? I'm not daft. He was probably a white slave trader or a perv or something… Only it was time for me to have a midlife crisis wasn't it? Before I lost the chance.

My friend Mandy she had the top of her ear pierced. Me, I knocked on the door of number 43…

And I stayed there for two whole weeks and I didn't call work or friends or family. The police kicked up a hell of a stink when I re-appeared and just resumed my old life, bold as brass. They still don't know where I was or what I did, well it's none of their business is it?

I've still got a place there at number 43, I drop by occasion-ally for a long weekend when I need a break from my ordi-nary okay life. I still share a table with him at the café some-times too, he sketches and I read my trashy novels and we don't talk. We don't need to...

Wild Life

Her phone pinged into life at 6.30am, a tinkly alarm to call her from sleep.

She sprang out of bed, leaving Tim fast asleep, he never heard her alarm and had his own set for 8.

She threw on Tim's robe and headed downstairs, she switched on the kettle and muttered under her breath "today is my day".

As she practised her morning yoga poses she thought through her schedule. Exercise completed, she poured warm water onto a slice of lemon and then grabbed some yoghurt and blueberries from the fridge and sat down to write her thoughts. Her journaling completed, Caroline read a couple of pages of her latest improving book.

7.00am and Caroline jumped into the shower.

7.15 saw her pulling on blue jeans, a shirt carefully tailored to look decidedly casual and slipping into her most comfortable black heels.

By the time Tim was coming around Caroline was at her desk in their shared office checking her emails.

She threw her notebook, diary and laptop into her bag and headed for her meetings in the city. Knowing that there would be no good places to park her car, she jumped on a bus and started listening to one of her favourite podcasts.

She had productive meetings with two of her least hated clients, the sort who listened to what she had to say, took her advice and paid her on time.

She was due to meet her friend Lizzie for lunch, but she had enough time to check her emails and complete a couple of quick writing jobs.

There were a few new clients and deadlines in her inbox so she updated her diary, it was pretty full for the next six months, she might need to think about turning new work down soon.

Her work done, Caroline packed her bag and headed for the restaurant. She loved these monthly catch-ups with Lizzie, work was a no-go topic, this lunch was men, gossip and trashy tv. She got to the restaurant first, she always did, Lizzie was late for everything. Caroline usually had a glass of white zinfandel before her friend arrived, but this time she ordered fizzy water. This puzzled her, but she went with it, it was refreshing.

Lizzie arrived, but she looked a bit odd. She was apologising as usual for being late 'due to reasons', but Caroline was having trouble seeing her properly, it was like her mouth was moving out of synch to the sound she was making. Caroline blinked. Maybe she was tired, she'd had a few bad nights recently, she could do with a quiet weekend she thought.

They ordered their usual, thank goodness they were well-known in the restaurant because Caroline couldn't quite remember what her usual was. When the food came it was disappointingly tasteless and what she could only describe as 'fuzzy around the edges'.

Caroline wondered whether it was time to get her eyes tested again, maybe she needed a stronger prescription? Her current lenses didn't seem to be cutting it any more. The phone on the table in front of her lit up and began to tinkle. Caroline looked down, slightly confused, why was her phone playing the morning alarm tune?

Caroline felt funny, like she was dropping from a great height. She hated this, it was like she was waking from a very vivid dream, but how could that be?

She opened her eyes. She was in bed, tangled up in the duvet, as always. Tim lay next to her, breathing softly, the duvet neatly spread over him. Caroline grabbed her phone and peered at the screen, "welcome to lockdown day eleventy hundred", it mocked.

Be

"Be", he says.

"Be what?" She says.

"Authentic", he says.

She's standing on a stage in jeans and a jumper, his jumper actually, though he won't have noticed. She's rehearsing a play. His play actually, he wrote it and is now directing it and he demanded; demanded mind, that she was the star.

"Authentic to what?" She says.

"Well, to Molly's motivations." He says.

"And what are Molly's motivations?" She says.

Why? Why say that? She knows what he's going to say next...

"What do you think they are?" He says.

Fuck. Why did she have to start this again?

"I don't know, I guess she's fed up, he's got this new job that he's all fired up about and she's feeling like she's not the centre of his world any more."

"Right", he says. "And so how does that make her behave?"

“Well”, she says, “she’s used to it happening, so she just gets on with her own life and pretends she doesn’t care what he’s doing. Only something’s different this time, something’s changed.”

“Really?” He says. “What’s changed? The new job isn’t that different from the last few jobs he’s had, why does she think this one’s different?”

Why’s he asking her? It’s not fair, he wrote the thing, he must know what his character’s feeling. He does have the reputation as a director of really wanting his actors to get under the skins of their characters, so this is probably just an exercise and when she’s had her say he’ll go ‘that’s really interesting, but that’s not what I had in mind at all’, pretentious prick…

“Okay”, she says. “Maybe she thinks that this time he seems a lot more invested in the job, like he’s a lot more into it than anything he’s done for a while. Maybe she thinks that he’s putting a lot of energy into it because he’s trying to impress someone with what he’s capable of. Maybe he’s looking for a way out of a relationship he’s not happy with by creating something with somebody else...”

Her words hang in the air. She’d been aware of her voice rising as she said the last bit, aware of the emotion the words contained. She waits for his reply…

“That’s really interesting”, he says.

“Go on then, what did you have in mind?” She says.

“It’s not working is it.” He almost shouts it, “It’s not the same. She doesn’t get me, always phoning to see what I’m doing, always wanting to know what time I’ll be home or why she can't come and see me at work. I never had this problem wi..." His voice trails off.

"You never had this problem with me?" She says. "Well I had my own life didn't I. I had my own name and my own projects. We came to it as equals and we were happy to share what we had with each other. Did you write this for her really?"

"God no, she wouldn't be able to do this, this requires a woman who knows who she is and what she's about, it isn't a young woman's part. I really thought I had something with her you know, I thought she saw me as more than a meal ticket."

"Only interested in the size of your wallet is she?" It was a cheap dig, but she had been hurt when she was unceremoniously traded in for a younger model. "Did you let her read for this?"

"She saw a bit of it when I was writing it, said it just sounded a bit depressing and she thought kitchen dramas had had their day."

"What's a kitchen drama?"

"Something that Ozzy Osbourne wrote in 'the olden days', apparently". His face broke into 'that' smile.

She laughed, she couldn't help it.

"Oh you poor bugger, what did you say?"

"Well there was no point trying to correct her or explain was there? She's all over being 'in the now' at the moment, she doesn't like looking to the past, she doesn't think it has anything to teach us. Anyway, then she said she didn't think 'my sort of play' would be of interest to her 'target demographic' and that she couldn't see why anyone would bother dragging out to Stratford to see a play anyway, there couldn't be a very big theatre there...

Anyway, she packed her bags then, said she was going back to her mum's and if I ever wrote anything that was any good to give her a call..."

"Oh God, I'm really sorry."

"Well, it wasn't working anyway, she was always hogging the limelight, even when it wasn't her gig. I couldn't get a look in with the press on the BAFTA red carpet, she kept pushing in front of me and babbling about her latest podcast or Insta post. To be honest I had no idea what she was on about most of the time and I was bloody fed up of her photographing my dinner every night before she'd let me eat it.

You with anyone at the moment?"

Really? Not a very subtle approach. She could lie of course, there was that American actor she was going to the Leicester Square premiere with, but they'd been mates forever and there'd never been anything romantic in it.

"Me? No. I'm hardly in one place long enough at the moment. Spend most of my life on trains between Cardiff and Manchester and London, I've not really got any time to cultivate a new relationship." She said

"How about cultivating an old one?" He asked.

“Let’s take it from the top shall we?” She said grabbing her script…

“Are you serious?” He says. “You actually think we can just work together like nothing happened?”

“Oh no.” She says “It’s because we have that past that we can work together. I know exactly what you want and I’ll give it to you...”

He licks his lips, hungrily. He remembers…

“So come on,” she says. “Where do you want to start from? We need to make the most of these last few rehearsal sessions.”

“We could break for lunch; a long leisurely one.” He says “We could bunk off and go back to my place.”

“I thought I could give Simon a call.” She says. “It’d be great to have an extra session with both of us here, I thought we really had something yesterday.”

“So no lunch?” He says.

“I brought a sandwich from home.” She says. “You said you wanted to make the most of today, so I thought a quick break, then crack on...”

“I’d rather go to bed with you.” He says.

She lowers the script and drags the glasses from the top of her head so she can get a proper look at him…

“You write really eloquently,” she says. “I love your writing, but in real life you communicate like… I dunno… your language has no class, no subtlety, you just come out and say stuff and it sounds crude and coarse.

Let me be really clear, I don't want to rekindle our relationship. I don't want to go to lunch with you and I most definitely don't want to go to bed with you. You're a great writer and a fantastic director, but you were a crap lover. End of."

"But we were good together!" He says. "The press loved us."

"And what did you write when we were together?" She says "Fuck all, because your mind wasn't on the job.

And what work did I do? Nothing of consequence, because I spent most of my time propping you up by doing guaranteed money, soulless, lowest common denominator, crowd pleaser jobs to facilitate you doing fuck all. I wasn't your partner, I was your enabler!"

"That's a bit harsh." He says. "The sex was always good. And the press loved us."

"Look, I love working on your plays, I quite enjoy you directing me, but that's as far as it goes, anything more than a professional relationship with you is professional suicide for me, so let's just drop it. I'm not coming back into your bed..."

They work. They thrive on the energy they produce together. They create a work of startling beauty and power in the rehearsal room. And then…

"We who are about to die salute you..." She thinks "We'd rather not die, of course, but you never know..."

“Oh my God! The press love us!” He says. “I never thought I’d see that piece come to life like that, exactly how I’d imagined it. Thank you.”

They embrace. The hug lasts a little longer than it should. They kiss, long, slow, deep, passionately…

“Let me know when you’ve written the next one.” She says as she walks away.

She does not look back.

He stares, following her disappearing form into the mist…

An idea pops into his head, he pats his pockets, searching for a pen...

Mind Noise

It was a whining mid-pitched drone. It was in his head constantly, even when he slept it no longer dimmed.

It had started with a bang. He couldn't seek professional help for it either. Seeking help would mean he'd have to explain what he'd done and a doctor would have no option other than to alert the police.

It was all Dave's fault. Tim had been friends with Dave since nursery school, when they'd clashed over wanting to play on the same tricycle. They'd ended up attaching a trolley to the back of it and then spent many happy hours bombing around the playground mowing down anyone who got in their way. Over the years they'd got into scrapes as Dave had encouraged Tim to scrump apples, skip school, shoplift, try smoking and drinking, have his first sexual encounter and buy a gun from some bloke down the pub. Tim was one of life's followers, if only he'd decided to follow what his gran would have described as a 'nice boy' like Kevin, then he might have ended up with a steady job and some prospects. Instead he followed Dave around like a besotted puppy and got into increasingly worrying 'scrapes'.

Dave dared him to fire his gun in public, said he should do it at the swimming baths where there'd be loads of people, it would be a right laugh in front of a big audience, would scare the bejesus out of them and they'd get away with it because everyone would be too scared to speak to the police. Only Dave's a bit dopey isn't he? He said they should do it midweek, Wednesday lunchtime, but it's a school day, so the kids aren't there and it's 'Pensioners Special' day in the local caf, so all the oldies are there instead of swimming up and down the pool.

So Tim and Dave arrive at the baths and it's dead, absolutely empty, no audience at all. Instead of just turning 'round and going home Tim gets into a rage and fires his gun into the empty, echoey space…

The bang had made his ears ring, he hadn't really thought through the advisability of firing a gun in a swimming baths. Tim had assumed his ears would stop ringing eventually and they had, but the buzz had started in his head and then it had turned into this whine and now it just wouldn't stop. Needing to avoid medical professionals, Tim had done the twenty-first century thing and Googled his symptoms. It had not helped. He would have to come up with an alternative plan.

He would have to 'self-medicate' to try to resolve the problem. He wasn't entirely sure what he was going to do, but he realised that it would probably have to be quite radical.

The police had paid him a visit, of course they had, he and Dave had legged it out of the baths pretty quickly after he'd fired the gun, but the girl on reception had seen them. Tim had managed to talk his way out of it, they clearly didn't have anything on him, certainly not enough to ship him off to the cells. He had bought himself a bit of time. But the whining in his head went on…

He tried to lie down and sleep, but he couldn't make it quiet, he had to play music to distract his mind from the whine, so there was no rest. His research suggested that there was no cure for what he'd inflicted on himself but he wasn't prepared to believe that, there had to be a way…

He called Dave, he didn't know who else to speak to. They agreed to meet back at the swimming baths. Tim took his gun.

"What are you planning?" Asked Dave.

"I figure if I do it again it might reverse the problem, stop the whining in my head," Tim explained.

"Are you mad? D'ya not think it'll just make it twice as bad?"

Dave might have a point of course, Tim just knew that he was really tired and he wanted to sleep.

Tim raised his gun, he was ready to fire off one shot when he was struck by an interesting thought. Of course it would be mad to fire the gun into an echoey room, that would just double the whine like Dave said, but what if he fired the gun into something soft, so that it didn't have the chance to make too much noise?

He turned to face Dave…

The sound was certainly different this time, just a sort of wet thump. Tim didn't kill him, he's not an idiot — he's also not a very good shot, he got him in the shoulder. Dave explained to the police that it was just an accident, they accepted it, of course they did.

And Tim? The noise in his head didn't stop, of course it didn't, but worrying about how much trouble he might get into for shooting Dave certainly took his mind of it; for a while at least.

Ten Past One And I'm Not Eating Lunch

Ten past one and I'm not eating lunch. I scowl at the clock. Lunch is supposed to be from one to one forty-five, but I'm still at my desk. What's the point of having a timetable if you don't stick to it?

Forty five minutes I'm due for lunch and I won't be doing myself out; I shall take my full allocated time. But that'll put me out as well, of course, because I shan't be back until five to now.

I take my time over my lunch, Thursday is a ham and pickle sandwich and a banana. I drink my coffee and then wash up my plate and mug. I'm back at my desk at five to two.

I quickly check the emails, but there's nothing there that needs dealing with so I ignore the inbox and get on with the next task on the list.

There are three stories to edit. I don't know why he bothers, my employer I mean, he 'writes' these stories, supposedly keenly observed pen portraits of ordinary life and then sends then to me for polishing. The only thing I've ever seen him keenly observe is his bank balance, he can account for every penny. He does not keenly observe anything about life outside his own little bubble, that's what I'm for. That and keeping him on the straight and narrow.

Anyway, I have these three stories to 'edit'. What he does is, he has a vague idea about a character and a situation which he writes down. He sends then to me for what he calls the ‘colour’, that means the details, the action, the outcomes. I send them back to him and he fiddles about with the sentence structure and some of the words and then he gets me to send them off to his editors and publishers.

They, in their turn, get very excited about his new stories and publish them, paying him vast sums of money for the privilege. In his turn, he pays me vast sums of money for being his P.A.

I edit the three stories. It takes me a couple of hours because they’re all a bit sparse. Judging by the stains on the paper it was a red wine night when he had these ideas. He always drinks red wine when the wife’s away, that’ll be why these stories are a bit maudlin as well. Still, he’s done well to keep her, she’s only 22 and him pushing 60. They met when she was 18 and cast in one of his plays. One of his better ones, from when he was young and hungry and still out in the world. I think originally she really was fascinated by him, he is an interesting man, done lots of things in his time. Of course he’s charming, he took her out to dinner just to be polite and ended up bedding her because he was lonely. His wife at the time had totally lost interest in him and had gone off with his credit card on a trip to find herself. And she did. In the bed of a millionaire in Hollywood.

So anyway, divorce and wife number two followed. For a while he got his spark back, started going out again and writing some really good stuff, but it didn’t last.

He got it into his head that she was having an affair with her co-star, who, bless him, is gay and happily married to a man named Bob. Anyway, his nibs had a tantrum and then spiralled into one of his states again, just when the diary was full of work. We had literature festivals up to our eyeballs, constantly on trains because we ‘don’t do flying’. He would do flying, but then he'd have to learn how to do his own travel bookings, so that isn't going to happen.

So, I got him away, doing the rounds of the festivals and a bit of telly and radio too. Took his mind off the fact that he thought she was having an affair.

I told her to leave off calling him for a few days and make sure she was seen out and about. Said I'd text when he'd calmed down a bit.

Well, by three days in he was all sweetness and light again, so I gave him his phone back and told him to ring and apologise, which he did. By the time we got back from our little tour, plus a long weekend in Blackpool to visit my sister, they were back to being love's young dream.

By the time I've finished the stories he's wandered in with a couple of ideas for blog posts. I say ideas, they're mostly just titles or random words, but I know what he means, so I crack on and start writing them. Sometimes he joins me in my office and lobs a few thoughts at me. I jot them down to be polite, but I edit them out later once he's wandered off again. I work on the blog posts until I get bored of his voice, if I'm lucky I can get four or five done ready to type up another day.

He sends me a folder of photos every day so I can choose what goes on his social media. He's getting quite good at taking decent pictures, certainly enough to share with his fans and followers.

He brings in the post for me to send on my way home. He's always been very good about dealing with the mailbag, you can guarantee that if you write to him the response will genuinely come from him. I can do his signature, I practice from time to time, but I've never signed anything in his name.

He's on tv tonight, one of those interviews on a sofa about his new series, well the one he's written, he won't act again he says. He says that every few years, then has a few years when he doesn't even talk about acting, then he writes a piece that it's obvious no one else could do justice to, then he walks back on stage like he's never been away. He wants to know which tie he should wear. I tell him not to wear one, unbutton two buttons on a clean white shirt and relax. He fusses about his hair, so I get the special scissors and trim it a bit. I've cut his hair for the last forty years, he's always complimented on his hair.

And now it's four thirty, time for me to pack up for the day so I can get to the Post Office on my way home. I remind him that I won't be in until ten tomorrow because it's Friday. He smiles and says he doesn't know what he'd do without me. He's been saying that for forty years.

I close the door and walk away. I don't look back, I never do. He's just a job, nothing to do with my life. He doesn't even know my husband's name is Henry.

About The Author

Sarah is a writer, storyteller, poet and performer, who creates works to inspire and connect her and her readers to the world.

When she's not writing, she's reading, gardening, annoying her cat, or running.

She divides her time between Newport and Edinburgh.

Special Thanks To…

Adrian, Jonathan, Jo, Leo, mum and dad, and the Genius who grabs the good ideas and plants them in my head.

www.ingramcontent.com/pod-product-compliance
Ingram Content Group UK Ltd.
Pitfield, Milton Keynes, MK11 3LW, UK
UKHW020233250726
13967UKWH00001B/341

9 781716 599163